ZERAFFA GIRAFFA

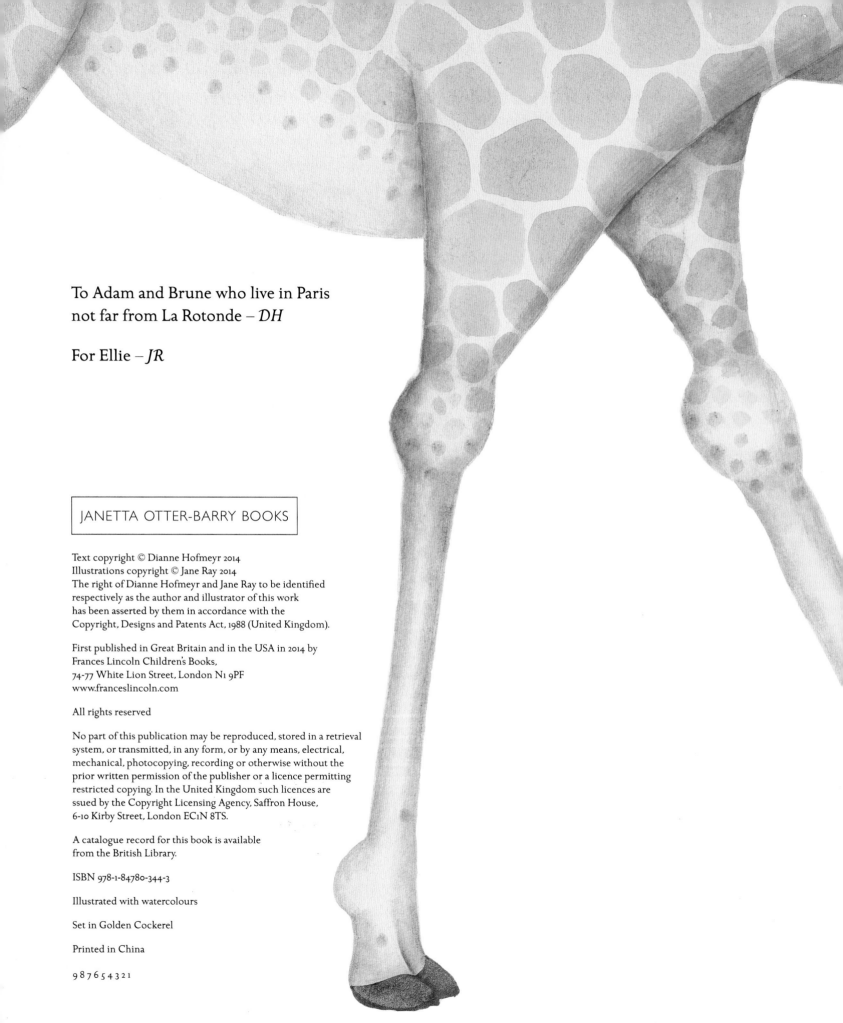

To Adam and Brune who live in Paris
not far from La Rotonde – *DH*

For Ellie – *JR*

JANETTA OTTER-BARRY BOOKS

Text copyright © Dianne Hofmeyr 2014
Illustrations copyright © Jane Ray 2014
The right of Dianne Hofmeyr and Jane Ray to be identified
respectively as the author and illustrator of this work
has been asserted by them in accordance with the
Copyright, Designs and Patents Act, 1988 (United Kingdom).

First published in Great Britain and in the USA in 2014 by
Frances Lincoln Children's Books,
74-77 White Lion Street, London N1 9PF
www.franceslincoln.com

A catalogue record for this book is available
from the British Library.

ISBN 978-1-84780-344-3

Illustrated with watercolours

Set in Golden Cockerel

Printed in China

9 8 7 6 5 4 3 2 1

ZERAFFA GIRAFFA

DIANNE HOFMEYR

Illustrated by JANE RAY

F

FRANCES LINCOLN
CHILDREN'S BOOKS

Across the plains of Africa where grass grows tall and acacias taste sweet, came the hunters from the Great Pasha of Egypt and the Sudan.

When they captured a small giraffe, no taller than the tallest of them, they tied her in a sling to the side of a camel and kept her alive on camel's milk on the journey home.

The Pasha was delighted.

"She is the perfect gift for my friend, the King of France!"

He appointed his servant boy, Atir, as her keeper and handed him a letter addressed to the King, along with a map.

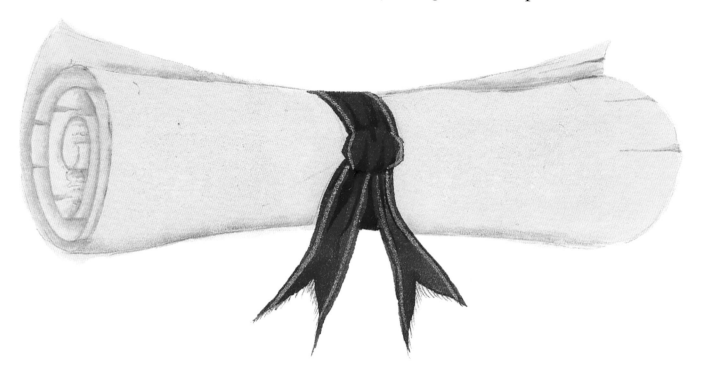

Atir unrolled the map and measured the distance.
Paris was very far away. It was beyond the edge of Africa, over the sea on the other side of the world.

But first they had to sail down the River Nile.

A *felucca* was built, with two elegant sails that see-sawed and pivoted to catch the breeze, with an awning to protect the little giraffe from the sun.

"I'll name you Zeraffa," Atir whispered
as he hung an amulet around her neck.
"I'll feed you milk sweet as lake water,
and at night I'll roll back the awning
so you can look at the stars."

Out past the markets of Khartoum
they sailed, with the hot *haboob*
wind filling their sails... past the
silent giraffe paintings of Luxor...

past the lion-faced Sphinx
and her Pyramids.

They sailed past ladies combing
their hair with porcupine quills
who offered them dates
and pomegranates...

until they came to the place
where the sea sipped up the Nile.

Atir led Zeraffa on board a boat bound for France.
And at night the sailors sang songs to the
beautiful long-necked creature that gazed down
at them from between the sails.

On the cobblestones of Marseilles, people pushed
forward for a glimpse of her.
The Mayor threw up his hands when Atir told him
he needed to travel to Paris.

"With a giraffe? How? It's impossible! We must consult
Monsieur Stravganza, inventor of things *extraordinaire*."

So Monsieur Stravganza drew sketches.
He added a propeller here, an extra wheel there.
But each time, the Mayor shook his head.

"No! A machine like that will never work."
"A giraffe carried by a hot air balloon? Impossible!"
"We can walk," said Atir.
"But Paris is 550 miles away!"
"Zeraffa has long legs," said Atir.

So they set off with guards on horses, a carriage,
two milk cows and Atir leading Zeraffa, protected
by a waxed taffeta cloak.
They walked through orchards of almonds and olives. . .
through fields of red poppies. . .

through the vineyards of the Rhone valley,
where the mistral wind blew so cold that
the waxed taffeta cloak had to be replaced
with a woollen one trimmed with fur.

News of the amazing creature soon spread.
In Lyon, hundreds of people turned out
to see her.

By the time they neared Paris, thousands were
lining the road, greedy for a glimpse of her.
  "It's the creature from Africa!"
  "Zeraffa of Africa!"
  "Zeraffa Giraffa!"

Children squeezed through the crowds
to count her spots. Ladies leant from salon
windows to tickle her ears.

But Zeraffa took no notice.
She strolled down the Champs-Élysées,
nibbling the tops of the trees just as
she had done on the plains of Africa.

Paris

At the palace of Saint-Cloud the Queen organised
a *soiree*. Guests gathered in bristling uniforms
and rustling taffeta to admire Zeraffa.

"What a handsome creature!" exclaimed the gentlemen.
"How sweet she is!" sighed the ladies.
"Such long eyelashes!"
"Such a black tongue!"

In the *Jardin des Plantes*, the King had prepared
a Rotunda with wooden floors and a mosaic of straw
on the walls. People came in their thousands to see her.

Paris fell in love.
They wrote poems and songs.

Gardeners clipped giraffe hedges.
Bakers baked giraffe biscuits.
Dogs wore spotted jackets. Men wore tall hats.
Girls wore red ribbons around their necks.

Ladies glued long eyelashes to their lids and twisted
their hair up into styles *á la Girafe*. . . so high they had
to lie down inside their carriages as they rode across
Paris to see her.

In the evenings, after the crowds had left,
the King's granddaughter,
Louise Marie Thérèse, slipped
secretly into the garden. She climbed
the ladder to the platform,
where she stood face to face
with Zeraffa and combed
her mane and fed her apples.

Then she listened as Atir whispered in Zeraffa's ear.
He told tales of a hot land far away where grass grows
tall and acacias taste sweet.

He whispered stories of a lake and of stars
that turn the sky into curdled milk,
and of a hot *haboob* wind.

Then they stood in silence and looked out
over the lights of Paris. And on those evenings,
when the air was particularly balmy,
all three turned their faces southwards. . .
and on the warm air they felt the kiss of Africa.

ABOUT THE REAL ZERAFFA

Muhammad Ali was a fierce ruler in Egypt who wanted to make friends with the King of France, Charles X. When he heard that the King was planning a collection of strange animals, he decided a giraffe would be the perfect gift.

A baby giraffe was captured on the plains of Africa in 1824, but she was too weak to walk and so was strapped to a camel and taken to the banks of the river Nile. The giraffe was loaded onto a small boat called a *felucca* and taken down the river all the way to the Mediterranean Sea. Here, she was loaded onto a bigger sailing ship and taken across the sea to Marseilles in France. But when she arrived, nobody knew how the giraffe would get all the way to Paris where the King lived. Eventually, it was decided she would walk.

The entire journey, starting with her being tied to a camel, the 2,000-mile trip down the Nile, the three-week sail across the Mediterranean Sea and finally the 550-mile walk from Marseilles to Paris, took two and a half years. By the time she arrived in Paris, she stood four metres tall and was the first giraffe ever seen in France. The year was 1827.

She lived with her keeper, Atir, in a building called *La Rotonde* in the *Jardin des Plantes*. Atir slept high up on a platform, close to her face, and never left her side. Twelve years later a second young female giraffe was transported down the Nile and sent to Paris to keep her company. When Zeraffa died of old age on 12 January, 1845, after living in Paris for 18 years, Atir was still with her.

La Rotonde still stands in the *Jardin des Plantes* and if you visit on a quiet day and close your eyes, perhaps you'll feel the hot wind and imagine yourself there with Zeraffa, Atir and Louise Marie Thérèse.